DAVID CONWAY was born in Ireland but moved to England as a baby,
and has lived there ever since. He currently works at home, bringing up
his daughter and son, and writing for children. David is the author
of a number of picture books including *The Most Important Gift of All*,
illustrated by Karin Littlewood. *Lila and the Secret of Rain*
won a US Spring 2008 Parents' Choice Gold Award
and is his first title for Frances Lincoln.

JUDE DALY lives in Cape Town, South Africa with her husband, writer
and illustrator Niki Daly. Her recent books for Frances Lincoln include
To Everything there is a Season, The Little Blue Slipper, The Elephant's Pillow
by Diana Reynolds Roome, winner of a US Parents' Choice Silver Award,
The Faraway Island by Dianne Hofmeyr, *Let There Be Peace*
and *Sivu's Six Wishes*.

For Jude, love Dad – D.C.
For Joe, with love – J.D.

Lila and the Secret of Rain

David Conway

Illustrated by Jude Daly

F

FRANCES LINCOLN
CHILDREN'S BOOKS

For weeks and weeks the sun beat down
on the Kenyan village where Lila lived.

It was very hot, so hot that Lila, her mama
and brother, and all the other villagers stayed
in their houses to keep away from the burning sun.

It was too hot to gather firewood,

too hot to weed

the village garden,

and even too hot to milk the cow.

One night Lila overheard her mama talking about the well
that had dried up and the crops that were failing.
"Without water there can be no life," Lila heard her mama say.

Lila wanted so much for the sun to stop shining
and for the rain to come.
But the sun did not stop shining and the rain did not come.

One evening Lila's grandfather
told her a story about a man
that he'd met once when he was
a boy – a man who had told him
the secret of rain.
"You must climb the highest
mountain," said the man to Lila's
grandfather, "and tell the sky
the saddest thing you know."

Lila listened very carefully
to what her grandfather said.
The following morning
when the sun was still asleep,
Lila left the village and
set off to find the highest
mountain she could.

Lila walked and walked
and walked, and at last
she found herself at the foot
of a very tall mountain.

Lila began to climb,
higher and higher
and higher.

When Lila reached
the top of the mountain
she began to tell the sky
the saddest things she knew.

First, she told of the time her brother cut his leg
while chasing a chicken in the village.
Then she told of the time she burned her fingers
while helping her mama to cook.

On and on Lila went, telling the sky the saddest things she knew. At the end of each one she looked to the sky for a sign of rain, but the sky remained blue and the sun still shone very brightly.

Lila began to cry.

"What can I do?" she said to the sky.

"It is too hot to collect firewood,
too hot to weed the village garden,
and too hot to milk the cow.
The well is dry and the crops are failing.
Without crops there will be no food,
without food the people in the village
will become sick, and without water
there can be no life."

Everything on the mountaintop was silent.
Nothing could be heard except the sound of Lila weeping.

Then a breeze began to blow and the dust
around Lila's feet started to dance.
Clouds began to fill the sky like flocks of white birds,
slowly blocking out the sun's scorching rays.

The clouds grew darker and darker, filling with Lila's sadness…
until the sky was ebony with emotion.

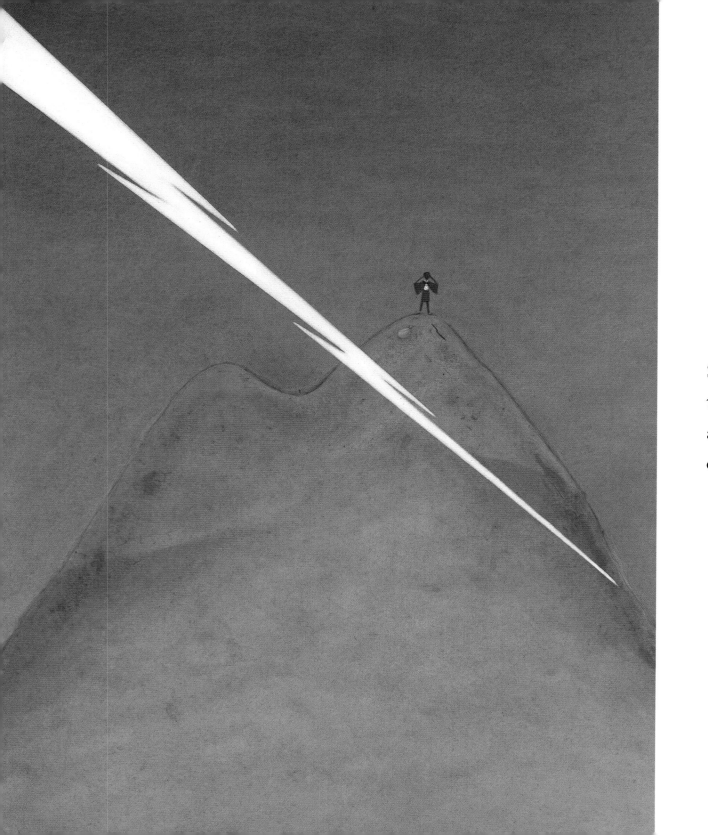

Suddenly a flash of lightning
tore across the sky and
a loud roar of thunder
echoed around the mountain.

Lila felt the gentle touch
of a raindrop on her foot...

then another
and another and another

until the ground was awash
with tears of rain.

Lila joyfully lifted up her hands to the crying sky,
for each raindrop felt like one of her mama's kisses.

As fast as she could, Lila ran down the mountain.

By the time she reached home,
all the villagers were celebrating
the rain with music and dancing.

Lila's mama was very relieved to see her home again
safe and sound. She hugged her close while
Lila's grandfather gave her a knowing smile…

for only Lila and her grandfather
knew that she had saved the village
with the secret of rain.

MORE TITLES ILLUSTRATED BY JUDE DALY
FROM FRANCES LINCOLN CHILDREN'S BOOKS

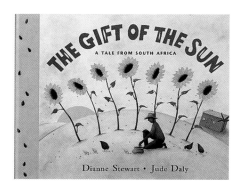

The Gift of the Sun
Dianne Stewart
Illustrated by Jude Daly

When Thulani tires of milking the cow, he exchanges it for a goat… the goat for a sheep… the sheep for three geese … until all he has left is a pocketful of sunflower seeds! But the seeds feed the hens, the hens lay more eggs than ever, and soon Thulani is enjoying the gift of his newfound fortune.

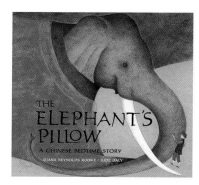

The Elephant's Pillow
A Chinese Bedtime Story
Diana Reynolds Roome
Illustrated by Jude Daly

The Imperial Elephant hasn't slept a wink since the old Emperor died. Sing Lo decides to find out why, and discovers that a curious riddle, a silk cushion, and more must be dealt with before the elephant's problem is solved… A story for all children who have their own special bedtime rituals.

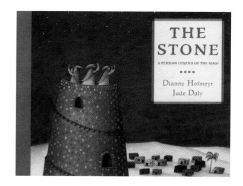

The Stone
Dianne Hofmeyr
Illustrated by Jude Daly

In the Persian town of Saveh, three astronomers see a fiery new star and link it with an ancient legend prophesying the birth of a remarkable baby. The wise men set off to honour the child with gifts, and in return he gives them a mysterious box containing a stone… A thought-provoking story retold from the 13th-century journal of the Venetian traveller Marco Polo.

Frances Lincoln titles are available from all good bookshops.
You can also buy books and find out more about your favourite titles,
authors and illustrators on our website: www.franceslincoln.com